Nelly's Grannies

BY ELIZABETH SLOTE

Tambourine Books New York

And so they were. There was the little brown house and the big blue pond. And there was Granny Gussy, wearing her prettiest apron.

"My little onions!" she cried, kissing and hugging them.
She smelled like flowers and hay.
Granny Gussy was tall and skinny like Nelly's father,
with the same freckles. He called her Mother and
she called him Nestor.

Right away, Nelly jumped into the pond and swam.
"I see you," yelled Granny Gussy, waving.

She made them a scrumptious
dinner of corn and tomatoes and
blueberry pie with ice cream.
When it got dark she showed Mike
and Nelly the stars, and the pictures
they made in the sky. She told them
stories of long ago and sang to them
in her trembly voice.

Nelly lay in her bed, listening to the night.
Something called *whoo? whoo?*
"What's that?" she whispered.
"It's an owl," said Mike.
She heard frogs croaking and crickets
thrumming as she fell asleep.

When she woke up she saw Granny Gussy out
in the boat in the middle of the misty pond.
"What's she doing?" she asked Mike.
"Catching us a fish for breakfast, of course."

Sometimes they picked blueberries up on the hill.
"Watch out for poison ivy," Granny Gussy said.

Sometimes they walked into the village for sodas
and got a ride back in the hay truck.

There was always something to watch — fish guarding
their pebble nests, turtles napping in the sun, mysterious
bugs with stripes and dots.

Then one day Nelly's father said it was time to go.
"Now we are going to visit your granny Lou."
"But I don't want to go," Nelly cried.
"Be good, my little onions!" waved Granny Gussy.
Nelly waved back until they'd driven up over the hill
and she couldn't see her anymore.

Nelly sat on her mother's lap and soon saw lots of
interesting things. Big buildings appeared and then
bigger ones. They drove along a great river and by docks
where ocean-going ships lay, shining in the sun.
"Hey, we're almost to Granny Lou's house," she said.

There was Granny Lou, outside waiting for them,
wearing her best hat. "My precious jewels!" she cried,
hugging and kissing them. She smelled like perfume,
soap, and mothballs. She was soft and squishy, like
Nelly's mother.

While the grown-ups sat and talked, Nelly went over
to the window to see what the neighbors were up to.

That night, Granny Lou took them to a fancy restaurant
where a waiter brought Nelly a dessert that was on fire!

Granny Lou read to them at bedtime. She wore a sparkly hairnet and golden slippers and had pink goop all over her face. Beauty cream she called it, and let Nelly have some, too.

Nelly lay awake. "I miss the stars," she said to Mike.
"There aren't any stars in the city."
"But look," said Mike, "look at the lights." They watched
together and heard the night sounds — car horns and
music, sirens, people talking and laughing on the streets.

The next day Granny Lou took them on the subway

to the art museum.

They played in the park, ate ice cream, and
watched the busy streets.

Then one day her father said it was time for them all to
go back home.
"But I don't want to go!" cried Nelly.
Granny Lou gave her a big, squishy hug and waved
good-bye as they drove away through the busy streets.
When Nelly couldn't see her anymore, she cried.

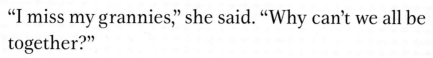

"I miss my grannies," she said. "Why can't we all be together?"

When they got home, Momma helped her write two letters, one to each granny:

Dear Granny,
Will you please come visit me soon?
Love,
NELLY

And they did!